W9-BVM-574

JP/TINY

Copyright © 1953 by Lois Lenski. Copyright renewed 1981 by Steven Covey and Paul A. Covey.
All rights reserved under International and Pan-American Copyright Conventions.
Published in the United States by Random House Children's Books, a division of
Random House, Inc., New York, and simultaneously in Canada by
Random House of Canada Limited, Toronto.
Originally published by Oxford University Press in 1953.
www.randomhouse.com/kids

Library of Congress Cataloging-in-Publication Data
Lenski, Lois, 1893–1974
On a summer day / by Lois Lenski. — 1st Random House ed.
p. cm.
SUMMARY: In rhyming text, a girl describes the many ways in which she and
her brother play together on a summer's day.
ISBN 0-375-82730-7 (trade) — ISBN 0-375-92730-1 (lib. bdg.)
[1. Play—Fiction. 2. Brothers and sisters—Fiction.] I. Title.
PZ8.3.L546On 2005 [E]—dc22 2004005591
MANUFACTURED IN MALAYSIA First Random House Edition

10 9 8 7 6 5 4 3 2

RANDOM HOUSE and colophon are registered trademarks of Random House, Inc.

ON A
SUMMER DAY

LOIS LENSKI

Random House 🏠 New York

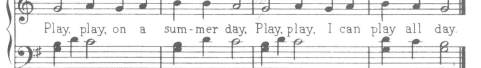

ON A SUMMER DAY

WORDS BY LOIS LENSKI
MUSIC BY CLYDE ROBERT BULLA

Play, play, on a sum-mer day, Play, play, I can play all day;

Out in the yard won't you come with me? Out in the yard is the place to be.

Play, play, on a sum-mer day, Play, play, I can play all day.

When we play *house*
　　I'm the mother of three;
Brother plays daddy
　　And takes care of me.

When we play *store*
   I come to buy;
Brother's the store man
   And prices are high.

Sometimes I'm a *lady*
  And put on long clothes,
Big shoes with high heels—
  I walk on my toes.

But Brother plays *Indian*
Back of a tree;
He lets out a war-whoop
To try to scare me.

And if we play *school*
　　At me he must look;
I am the teacher—
　　We read in a book.

When we play *church*
  There's always a crowd;
Brother's the preacher,
  He talks very loud.

When we play *auto*
  We go for a ride;
Brother can steer us,
  The sidewalks are wide.

When we play *train*
He makes it go,
With boxes for seats
All set in a row.

And if we play *horsie*
 Brother pulls me;
I call *Giddy-ap!*
 I say *Haw* and *Gee!*

When horsie gets hungry
I feed him some hay;
Then off on the grass
He gallops away.

When we play *dog*
   We crawl on our knees;
We bark very loud
   And growl all we please.

When doggie gets hungry
   I give him a bone;
He lies on the rug
   And chews till it's gone.

When we play *picnic*
   We swim in our pool;
We sail all our boats
   And keep nice and cool.

After our swim
   We sit in the shade;
We eat a good lunch
   And drink lemonade.

Sometimes we play *monkey*
And climb up a tree;
We look all around—
There's plenty to see.

When we play *band*
My horn I blow;
Brother beats his drum
And hop-step we go.

When Brother plays *elephant*
   I ride on his back;
I feed him some peanuts
   Out of my sack.

And if we play *hunter*
    We like to explore;
We find a dark cave
    With a wide open door.

Then we play *bear*
    And inside we creep;
All winter long
    We lie still and sleep.

At last we wake up
    As hungry as *bears;*
We gobble our luncheon
    Of cookies and pears.

And then we take turns
    Swinging up in a tree;
I push Brother
    And he pushes me.

And this is how
    We end our play—
We swing a while
    On a summer day.